The Dinky Donkey

For Maia. My beautiful girl.
— Craig Smith

To the gorgeously giggling Scottish Granny, who has touched
hearts across the globe with her laughter medicine, reading to the
adorable Archer and inspiring reading aloud to children worldwide.
And to Felicity... for being sent from heaven.
— Katz Cowley

Library of Congress Cataloging-in-Publication Data available

ISBN 978-1-338-60083-4

10 9   20 21 22 23

Printed in the U.S.A.   40
This edition first printing, November 2019

The artwork was created in watercolor, colored pencil, and stinky-inky pinkiness.
The text was set in Drawzing.

Book design by Smartwork Creative, www.smartworkcreative.co.nz

The Dinky Donkey

Words by **Craig Smith**

Illustrations by **Katz Cowley**

SCHOLASTIC INC.

NEW YORK TORONTO LONDON AUCKLAND
SYDNEY MEXICO CITY NEW DELHI HONG KONG

Wonky Donkey had a child . . .

it was a little girl.

Hee Haw!

She was so cute and small!

She was a **dinky** donkey.

Wonky Donkey had a child,
it was a little girl.

Hee Haw!

She was so cute and small . . .

and she had beautiful *long* eyelashes!

She was a
blinky dinky
donkey.

Wonky Donkey had a child,
it was a little girl.

Hee Haw!

She was so cute and small,
she had beautiful long eyelashes . . .

and she loved to listen to rowdy music.

She was a **punky** blinky dinky donkey.

Wonky Donkey had a child,
it was a little girl.

Hee Haw!

She was so cute and small,
she had beautiful long eyelashes,
she loved to listen to rowdy music . . .

and she painted her hooves bright pink.

She was an
inky-pinky
punky
blinky
dinky donkey.

Wonky Donkey had a child,
it was a little girl.

Hee Haw!

She was so cute and small,
she had beautiful long eyelashes,
she loved to listen to rowdy music,
she painted her hooves bright pink . . .

and she had to go pee-pee.

She was a **winky-tinky** inky-pinky
punky blinky dinky donkey.

Wonky Donkey had a child,
it was a little girl.

Hee Haw!

She was so cute and small,
she had beautiful long eyelashes,
she loved to listen to rowdy music,
she painted her hooves bright pink,
she had to go pee-pee . . .

and she loved to play the piano.

She was a **plinky-plonky** winky-tinky inky-pinky punky blinky dinky donkey.

Steinbray

Wonky Donkey had a child,
it was a little girl.

Hee Haw!

She was so cute and small,
she had beautiful long eyelashes,
she loved to listen to rowdy music,
she painted her hooves bright pink,
she had to go pee-pee,
she loved to play the piano . . .

and she wore wild sunglasses.

She was a **funky** plinky-plonky winky-tinky
inky-pinky punky blinky dinky donkey.

Wonky Donkey had a child,
it was a little girl.

Hee Haw!

She was so cute and small,
she had beautiful long eyelashes,
she loved to listen to rowdy music,
she painted her hooves bright pink,
she had to go pee-pee,
she loved to play the piano,
she wore wild sunglasses . . .

and she smelt just as bad
as her dad.

She was a **stinky** funky plinky-plonky winky-tinky inky-pinky punky blinky dinky donkey.

Wonky Donkey had a child,
it was a little girl . . .